THE MUMMY LIVES!

MARY LABATT

D1495268

Shea

KIDS CAN PRESS

Kids Can Press acknowledges the financial support of the Ontario Arts Council, the Canada Council for the Arts and the Government of Canada, through the BPIDP, for our publishing activity.

Published in Canada by
Kids Can Press Ltd.
29 Birch Avenue
Toronto, ON M4V 1E2

Published in the U.S. by
Kids Can Press Ltd.
2250 Military Road
Tonawanda, NY 14150

www.kidscanpress.com

Edited by Charis Wahl
Designed by Marie Bartholomew
Typeset by Rachel Di Salle

Printed and bound in Canada by Webcom

CM 02 0 9 8 7 6 5 4 3 2 1
CM PA 02 0 9 8 7 6 5 4 3 2 1

National Library of Canada Cataloguing in Publication Data

Labatt, Mary, date.
      The mummy lives!

(Sam, dog detective)
ISBN 1-55337-023-6 (bound)   ISBN 1-55337-042-2 (pbk.)

I. Title. II. Series: Labatt, Mary, date. Sam, dog detective.

PS8573.A135C87 2001   jC813'.54   C2001-900698-5
PZ7.L33Cu 2001

Kids Can Press is a Nelvana company

To Joanne and her family —
with my love

1. Another Boring Day

SNOW IS DISGUSTING.

Poking her head up under the lace curtain, Sam pressed her nose against the cold window. Wisps of snow swirled off the windowsill and drifted in front of the house.

Sam heaved a huge sigh. *What's a famous detective like me doing stuck in the house?*

She squinted at the snow-covered street. *I hate winter. All the good clues are buried. And everything smells like snow.*

Ice sticks between my toes. She threw herself back down on the couch to sulk. *I wish somebody would make me a pair of boots.*

Sam was alone because her owners, Joan and Bob Kendrick, were at work. All Sam could think about were endless winter days stretching ahead. Even Christmas would be boring. *That Santa guy must hate dogs. Last year he gave me a plastic bone. Nobody in their right mind would chew a plastic bone. What does he think I am ... stupid?*

After a while Sam went out to the kitchen to look for something to eat. *Hmph. You'd think they'd leave me a piece of cake or a few chips. Humans are so selfish.*

Then she remembered seeing a chocolate bar on Bob's dresser. She dashed upstairs, but it was gone. *Phooey. I can't believe how greedy Bob is.*

Hopping up on the spare bed, Sam settled down to dream about her favorite snacks. *I need a banana or jam sandwich ... or popcorn with ketchup ... or lemon pie with hot salsa ... or pizza with chocolate sauce.*

The only bright spot in Sam's dreary life was Jennie. Ten-year-old Jennie Levinsky was Sam's next-door neighbor and best friend. Joan and Bob hired Jennie to take Sam for walks when they were at work, and Jennie came every day after school.

When they met, Sam knew she'd found somebody to talk to. *I can always tell when someone's got the gift,* Sam had told Jennie. *Most dogs are too stupid to notice.*

Jennie was amazed. Sam's thoughts rang in her head like an echo. No one else could hear Sam, not even Jennie's best friend, Beth Morrison. And it was a secret. No one knew except the three of them.

Sam went back to the living room and looked out the window again. *Phooey. I can't find a good mystery in the winter. I can't spy on anybody. All the crooks stay inside. And everybody locks their windows.*

Sam watched an ice-covered car crawl around the corner. *Nothing happens in Woodford. If I don't find a mystery soon, I'm going to die of boredom. I need some excitement, and I need it bad.*

Just then something caught Sam's eye. Out of the snow came a strange figure. It was light gray, and its arms and legs were bumpy.

Sam snorted. *What's this? Looks like a huge worm.*

The figure came closer. *Hey! It's bald!* Sam struggled to see through the snow. The thing's head seemed to be white. *Hmm ... No hair and no face ...*

Sam's mind started to whir. *Definitely a worm ... Maybe someone dumped fertilizer on him and he grew and grew ...*

A picture of a mad scientist popped into Sam's mind. Bottles bubbled, long tubes carrying a glowing liquid snaked around the laboratory. Into the corners scuttled hairless mutants — people who had been changed by this strange potion. One looked like a giant bug, another like an alien, another like a worm ...

Hmmm ... Through the snow, Sam saw two black circles where eyes should be. *Very weird.*

Sam pictured the scientist again. Then she shrugged. *So there's a bunch of mutants walking* around. *Big deal. There's no mystery about that.*

The lumpy figure turned and fixed its eyeholes on Sam. Taking a little step toward her, it stretched out a lumpy arm.

Back off. Who invited you to visit?

Sam glared out the window. *You're no good to me, worm. I want a mystery. I never heard of a worm in a mystery.*

As the strange figure turned to go, it suddenly twisted around to look at Sam again. This time Sam could see that the eyeholes were black goggles. The thing craned its neck for a moment and stared.

Buzz off. I don't talk to worms. Do I look like a bird or something?

The figure turned and disappeared into the whirling snow.

Sam hopped off the couch in disgust. *There's nothing going on around here …*

Just some giant worm out for a walk.

2. The School Trip

An hour later Jennie and Beth burst in the front door.

"Sam!" cried Jennie. "We've got news!"

News is good. Sam raced down the stairs and licked at the two girls happily. Wiping their faces, they both laughed.

Sam sat down and looked up at her friends. *So, what's up?*

"We're going to the museum in the city!" Jennie brushed her long brown hair out of her eyes.

Sam stared.

"The museum, Sam! Our whole class is going!"

Are there good mysteries at the museum?

Jennie laughed. "It's not about mysteries, Sam. A museum is about history. There's loads of interesting stuff there."

Like what?

"Like dinosaur bones."

Yuck.

"Like Indian arrowheads."

The hair over Sam's eyes lifted. *Tell me you're kidding.*

"Sam's not impressed, Beth. What else is in the museum?"

"A stuffed buffalo!" Beth giggled, her green eyes sparkling.

A stuffed buffalo! Give me a break. You're getting excited about a stuffed buffalo and a bunch of old bones?

"Yeah. Miss Chong is taking our class on a field trip," said Jennie firmly.

Sam rolled her eyes. *Sounds as boring as my life.*

Jennie grinned. "Sam thinks it's boring."

Beth winked at Sam. "I bet I know what Sam

wants. She wants a new mystery."

You bet I do. I've got a whole winter ahead of me with nothing to do — and you two are yakking about some dead-bone place. Sam stared at Jennie. *Get me food.*

"Yes, Your Majesty," laughed Jennie. She raised her eyebrows at Beth. "Food, Beth. Get it now."

"Yes, sir!" Beth saluted.

Very funny. I'm hungry and I'm bored. I want pancakes with ketchup, nine chocolate cookies and some nacho chips with butterscotch sauce. Sam smacked her lips.

"Okay. Let's go." Jennie picked up her school bag. "We've got a whole pile of snacks at my house."

As Jennie was raiding the kitchen cupboards, her thirteen-year-old brother, Noel, walked in.

"Aha! Feeding that idiot dog junk food

again!" Noel glared down at Sam. "I'm telling Mom when she gets home from the drugstore."

Shut up, you great big teenage lummox.

"Junk food isn't for dogs," Noel said righteously. "It'll make her brain even smaller." He guffawed at his own cleverness.

Watch it, Oaf. Nice dogs like me have been known to bite.

Noel leaned his spiky blond head towards Sam. "Samantha, the walking garbage can."

Wrong, Lummox. It's Samantha, the world-famous detective.

"You shouldn't tease Sam, Noel," objected Jennie. "It might hurt her feelings."

Noel guffawed. "Dogs don't have feelings. They're dumb animals." He leered down at Sam. "Especially this one."

Sam glowered. *One little bite is all I want. Just one.*

Jennie closed her bedroom door firmly and spread chips and cheese puffs on the floor.

As Sam chomped and chewed and crunched, crumbs spewed out the sides of her mouth. *Life is looking up.* When she finished, she hopped up on Jennie's bed and belched.

"Miss Chong says we can choose our favorite part of the museum for our research project," Jennie said.

Now there's a thrill.

Beth hugged her knees like she always did when she was excited. "Maybe I'll do my project on dinosaurs!"

Wow. Call the TV station. This is news.

"I'm going to look at everything before I choose," said Jennie.

Yeah. Maybe they have some dried-up brains or some old toenails. Do a project on that.

But Jennie wasn't listening.

"I like arrowheads a lot," Beth mused. "Maybe ..."

Nobody likes arrowheads. Get a grip. What we need is a mystery.

But Jennie sill didn't hear.

Blah. Blah. Blah. Sam groaned and fell back on the pillows.

I've got two friends in this crummy town and they're both crazy.

They'd never find any excitement without me.

3. Finding out about Ancient Egypt

HMM ... LOOKS NICE AND SPOOKY.

The next day after school, Jennie, Beth and Sam lounged in Jennie's bedroom munching nachos and cookies.

Sam licked her chops and looked at Jennie hopefully. *These cheese nachos need some chocolate sauce.*

But Jennie was firm. "No chocolate sauce, Sam."

Phooey.

Beth started pulling books out of her schoolbag.

Sam's eyes narrowed in suspicion. *This looks like reading. I hate reading.*

Beth piled the books in front of her. "These are all about ancient Egypt. Miss Chong says that's the best part of the museum."

Sam glared. *I refuse to listen to reading.*

Beth opened the first book. "I've decided to do my project on Egypt."

Ask me if I care.

"Don't be so crabby, Sam," said Jennie. "Miss Chong said there's a mummy in the museum."

Why would they put somebody's mother in with a bunch of old bones?

"It's not somebody's mother!" laughed Jennie. "A mummy is a body that's been in an old tomb."

Great. More dead guys.

Beth pulled another book out of the pile. "Mummies are really interesting! Here's a book about them."

Sam groaned. *Don't let her start, Jennie. I hate it when this kid starts reading!*

"Sam doesn't want you to read, Beth." Jennie giggled, her brown eyes dancing.

"She'll love this." Beth grinned at the big dog.

"Wait until you hear what the ancient Egyptians did to people when they died!"

Who cares about dead people? I want some live crooks.

Jennie rolled her eyes.

Laughing, Beth opened the book and started to read. "First they took the body to a special place and washed it."

So they were clean. So what?

"Then they made a slit in the person's side and they pulled out the heart, the stomach, the intestines, the lungs and the liver."

Ugh. Revolting.

"Then they put all the organs in jars," Beth went on.

Jennie screwed up her face. "That's disgusting!"

Humans are always doing disgusting things.

"Listen to this!" squealed Beth. "They pulled the dead person's brain out through the nose with a hook!"

I think I'm going to throw up.

Jennie clutched her stomach, "Yuck."

"They thought dead people would need all their parts in the afterlife."

Sam lay back on the pillows. *Humans are so weird.*

Jennie made another terrible face. "Then what?"

"They wrapped the body in special bandages. When it's wrapped up it's called a mummy."

No dog would think this up. It's very sick.

Beth held up the book. There was a picture of a body laid out on a stone slab. Gathered around it were priests in white robes. Over their faces they wore masks of dogs and birds. Smoke rose from fires that cast long shadows on the stone walls.

"That's really spooky-looking," said Jennie.

Sam raised her head. *Hey! I like spooky stuff.*

Beth shivered. "You bet it's spooky. Those priests are chanting magic spells."

Sam sat up. *Magic is good.*

As Sam stared at the picture, her mind started to hum. *Looks like a perfect place for a mystery!* She saw herself going down steep, stone stairs to underground rooms. All around her were mummies stretched out on stone slabs.

There'd be ghosts in that place. Sam shivered happily. *I love ghosts.*

In her mind, Sam was creeping through the dark tomb, looking for ghosts.

She looked up at Jennie, the hair over her eyes rising and falling. *I've changed my mind. Ancient Egypt looks like a great place.*

Can I come to the museum, too?

4. Sam is Horrified

THOSE GUYS
WERE NASTY.

When Sam found out she couldn't go on the class trip, she was furious.

Did you ever notice how humans hog all the good stuff?

"But you told me you'd hate school," laughed Jennie. "You called it a prison for kids!"

Well ... I didn't know you talked about spooky stuff. I thought school was just reading and writing and junk like that.

"Guess what, Beth?" Jennie hooted. "Sam's getting interested!"

Grinning, Beth looked up from her book. "She's going to love the next bit! It gives me the creeps!"

Let's hear it.

"People are terrified to go into those tombs," said Beth darkly. "Some tombs have a curse on them!"

Sam shivered happily. *Curses are good.*

Jennie turned a page. "Hey! Look at all the stuff they put in the tomb with the mummy. Pottery, food, jewelry, silver ... gold."

Where there's treasure, there's robbers.

Sam pictured herself in the tomb. *I'm here to find out who's robbing this place. The king wants his treasure back. He's depending on me ... Sam, the great detective ... I'll catch the crooks when they come out. I'll be a hero. I'll have my picture in the newspaper.*

"Each tomb is deep under a pyramid," said Beth.

Jennie looked up. "So the pyramids are really tombs?"

"Yup." Beth read the rest of the page quickly. "They made burial chambers for kings and queens and then built pyramids over them. They're not the tombs of ordinary people."

Get back to the curses.

Beth ran her finger down the next page. "They put in all the things they thought the person would need and sealed the tomb. Then the priests cast a magic spell on it to scare thieves away."

Let's hear about those spells.

Beth flipped several pages. "Wow!"

I love this! Ghosts ... curses ... robbers ...

"Listen to this! The mummy took his favorite pets with him to the afterlife!"

Pets?

Jennie's eyebrows shot up. "What?"

"Yeah. The ancient Egyptians liked cats, but some of them had dogs."

Dogs are good. Nobody in their right mind would want a cat.

"If the person liked a pet," read Beth, "the priests killed it. Then they made a mummy out of it, too."

Sam gasped.

"And they put it in the tomb with its owner."

Wait a minute! Sam sat bolt upright on the

bed. *Those creeps killed dogs and made them into mummies?*

Jennie nodded. "Yup."

Suddenly Sam felt dizzy.

Beth read aloud. "Cats and dogs and monkeys were made into mummies, just like their people."

Sam began to see spots before her eyes. *Don't read any more. Cats deserve it ...*

Sam's head spun. *Monkeys probably deserve it, too.*

But not dogs!

5. The Mummy's Curse

WHITE DOG! THAT'S ME!

The day of the class trip finally arrived. Jennie had warned Sam that she'd be late for their walk.

Grumbling to herself, Sam paced the empty house. That morning Joan and Bob had tried to feed Sam dog food. Now a bowl of dried Liver Delight was stinking up the house.

Sam looked outside at the snow fluttering down in large flakes. There was no sound from the street.

I'm a world-famous detective and I've got no case. If I don't find one soon, I might bite somebody.

Sam sniffed the air disgustedly. *I think*

I'll practice on the next person who tries to feed me Liver Delight.

Sam dragged herself upstairs and flopped on the spare bed. *No dog ever had such a boring life. There should be a law about this.*

At last Sam heard the door key. *About time.* She dashed down the stairs and leaped on Jennie as she came through the door.

Sam licked and jumped and whined. *I've been waiting for hours!*

Jenny hugged Sam and hung her snowy coat on a hook.

Sam fixed Jennie with a hard stare. *Call the Humane Society and demand a better life for me. I never go anywhere. I never do anything.*

"We go for our walk every day."

Walks are dumb.

"All dogs like walks."

I'm not an ordinary dog. I'm a famous detective. Sam shot Jennie a nasty look. *Or did you forget?*

"Of course I didn't forget," giggled Jennie. "But I want to tell you about our trip to the museum. It was great!"

Did you find a mystery?

In Jennie's bedroom, Beth and Jennie chattered excitedly about the museum. Sam hopped up on Jennie's bed, and looked out at the worm thing striding down the empty street.

Boring!

She paced back and forth on the quilt. *Hurry up with the food.*

"We saw the mummy of a real pharaoh, Sam!" Jennie dished out Sam's popcorn and poured ketchup on it.

Sam gobbled some popcorn and looked up with ketchup-stained whiskers. *What's a pharaoh? Another dead guy?*

"A pharaoh is a king," answered Jennie. "We saw the mummy of Pharaoh Menopharsib the Fourth."

Big deal.

Beth shoved a handful of popcorn into her mouth. "Jennie and I are going to do our projects on Menopharsib!" Her red hair bounced and her green eyes blazed.

Sam stared at Jennie. *Who cares about projects? We need adventure.*

Jennie grinned. "Tell her something exciting, Beth."

Beth made a scary face. "There's a curse on Menopharsib's tomb! How's that?"

The hair over Sam's eyes lifted. *A curse is always good.*

"Yeah, Sam," Jennie went on. "And Pharaoh Menopharsib had a big white dog. There were pictures of him with his dog on the tomb wall."

Now Sam was interested. *Yeah?*

Jennie took a deep breath. "Guess what else?" *What?*

Jennie paused dramatically. "The writing said that the pharaoh wanted his dog with him in the afterlife."

Sam gasped. *Yikes! Did they make that poor dog into a mummy?*

"Yup," Jennie answered. "They buried Akasheput with Menopharsib and his treasure under a huge pyramid."

Sam shuddered. *Akasheput. Is that the dog's name?*

Jennie nodded, her brown eyes wide.

Sam dove under a pillow. *Don't tell me any more.*

"Menopharsib said he just couldn't go to the afterlife without his dog," Beth added through a mouthful of popcorn.

I guess they didn't have a Humane Society then.

Jennie folded her arms. "Wait until you hear about the spell the priests put on Menopharsib's tomb."

So, tell me.

Jennie leaned toward Sam. "The spell says that whoever broke into the tomb would die a terrible death!"

Sam pulled her head out from under the pillow. *Hmm ... I like spells ...*

"And the curse worked!" squeaked Beth excitedly. "The archaeologists who found the tomb died!"

Wow! What's an archaeologist?

"Someone who digs up old stuff." Jennie's brown eyes were wide. "The archaeologists went back to their hotel and in three days they all had a mysterious disease!"

Very spooky.

Beth chewed on a fingernail. "They broke out in a rash and died instantly!"

Whew! That's some spell.

Jennie dropped her voice to a whisper. "Want to hear what happened to Akasheput?"

I heard already. He got wrapped up.

"There's more. About a hundred years ago, thieves broke into the tomb and stole Akasheput's mummy. Nobody ever found it!"

Who'd want to drag some old dog around?

"Wait. You haven't heard it all."

I can't hear any more about this poor dog.

"The curse says that if anyone takes Akasheput out of the tomb, Menopharsib will walk the earth forever until he finds his dog!"

Oh ...

Beth started to pace. "That means he's walking the earth right now looking for his furry white dog!"

Sam stood up and danced back and danced forth on Jennie's bed. Under her feet the bedspread whipped into little swirls. In her mind she could see a rotting mummy wrapped in bandages, his eyes blind, roaming the earth and calling for his white dog. The magic of the ancient priests was with him. He could walk through walls. He could not be stopped by bullets ...

Suddenly Sam stopped dancing.

Hey! I'm big and white ... and furry.

I hope he doesn't come after me.

6. An Evil Pharaoh

I DON'T WANT THAT GUY NEAR ME.

During the next few days, Jennie's room filled with books and papers. Sam lounged on the bed demanding snacks as the girls talked about their research.

As she listened, the hair on the back of Sam's neck prickled. Menopharsib was an evil pharaoh, and his people were often killed by mysterious poisons. During his reign, Egypt lived in terror.

Menopharsib's priests were powerful. Known for horrible spells, they served their cruel master without question. Everyone feared them.

One of the books told about Menopharsib's

curse. Every person who had ever entered Menopharsib's tomb had died!

When the girls read about the way the priests created their curses, Sam almost fell off the bed. As part of their spells, Menopharsib's priests killed animals!

Did they sacrifice dogs? Sam felt woozy.

Jennie nodded.

But I thought Menopharsib liked dogs.

Jennie shrugged. "Maybe he only liked Akasheput."

Sam shuddered. *How did they do it?*

Jennie told Sam that the dog was tied to an altar and slit down the stomach.

I'm going to faint.

Jennie looked back at the last page she'd read. "The priests said their spells would last forever!"

Beth nodded. "Menopharsib's curse is supposed to kill anyone who disturbs his mummy. Even today."

Sam's head whipped up. *Wait a minute! You disturbed him!*

Jennie looked at Sam curiously. "What do you mean?"

All the kids in your class were gawking at him! That would disturb anyone.

"We all looked at him, Beth!"

Beth gulped. "H-he wouldn't like people staring at him, would he?"

A mummy would hate a whole bunch of kids pointing at him. I bet they made jokes and sick noises.

"N-nobody likes to be stared at," Jennie whispered.

This is dangerous. Sam pictured a huge mummy lumbering toward her, rotting bandages trailing from its arms and legs. Sam scrunched her eyes shut, but the mummy kept coming. Bony fingers reached out for her.

Jennie's mouth was dry. "I w-wish his mummy wasn't so close to Woodford."

"I wish we hadn't looked at him!" Beth chewed her fingernail.

"They should have l-left him in his t-tomb," Jennie said, twisting her long hair nervously.

That mummy probably put a spell on you.

You'd better check to see if you have a rash.

"Sam thinks we'll have the s-spell on us." Jennie lifted her top and peered at her stomach.

Beth chewed her fingernail harder.

Sam chortled quietly to herself. *Now we'll have some excitement ...*

Then a nasty thought hit her, and she looked down at her own stomach to see if she had a rash.

Hmm ...

Then she shrugged. *Hey ...*

Anything is better than being bored.

That evening, all Sam could think about were chanting priests in stone rooms deep under the ancient pyramids. Wearing the masks of bulls and birds, they tied dogs to stone altars. Dog mummies lined the walls.

Whew! Sam shook herself and hopped off the spare bed. *Those priests give me the creeps!*

Sam padded downstairs. *Maybe some fresh air will take my mind off this dog-mummy thing.*

She scratched at the front door and whined. Joan got up. "Do you want to go out, Sam?"

Sam whined again.

Joan opened the door. "Okay. But don't go far."

Sam stepped out into the cold night. Overhead the stars twinkled in the black sky, and white snow glistened all around her. She breathed deeply. *I can't smell anything but this stupid snow.*

Then Sam caught a whiff of something else. *Hey! Food!* She snuffled at the snow.

Ptooey! Snow clogged her nose. Then she smelled it again. Sniff. Sniff. Snuffle. Snuffle.

Sam nosed around the porch. *Aha!* Under a layer of fresh snow she found a piece of beef jerky.

Yum.

Wait a minute. A sudden thought hit Sam. *Who put this here?*

Then she shrugged. *Probably the mailman. He's*

always trying to make friends with dogs.

Sam sat down and chewed. *Very nice.*

When it was gone, she swallowed noisily and looked around. *So, where's the next one?* She nosed around the porch again, but the smell was gone.

Joan opened the door. "Time to come in, Sam."

Sam stepped back into the warm house.

Yum ...

I'm going to check that porch more often.

7. Will Menopharsib Come?

UH-OH, I CAN'T BITE A MUMMY.

Every day after school Jennie and Beth worked on their projects about Menopharsib. The more they talked about him, the more Sam felt his evil presence.

Sam's skin crawled as she leaned over to nibble at a piece of apple pie. *Don't forget that Menopharsib has magical powers. I bet he can hear everything you say.*

Jennie was busy drawing a title page for her project. It was called A Pharaoh and His Dog.

Sam stared at Jennie. *Magic, Jennie. That old pharoah can listen to us!*

Jennie looked up. "Sam thinks Menopharsib can hear us because he has magical powers."

Beth shivered. "But we have to talk about our projects. How else can we work?"

Watch what you say then. I don't want that guy mad at me.

"Sam wants us to be careful what we say."

Beth nodded. "Good idea, Sam."

"It's strange about his dog," Jennie said as she put the finishing touches on her drawing. "In ancient Egypt, dogs were skinny with short hair. But Akasheput was shaggy."

"I know why," said Beth, stapling her pages together. "Akasheput wasn't an Egyptian dog. One of the books said Menopharsib got him when they raided another country."

Did Akasheput look like me?

Jennie nodded. "Sort of. Here's a picture from one of the wall paintings." She held up a book.

Sam leaned over the edge of the bed.

That's a good-looking dog.

Beth held up her book. "And here's Menopharsib."

Sam peered at the picture. An evil pharaoh

glared back out of black-rimmed eyes. With hands folded across his chest, tunic of spotless white linen, jeweled arm band and colored headpiece, he stared out of the book across three thousand years.

Sam drew back. *Yikes! That guy looked right at me!*

"It's only a picture, Sam." But Jennie didn't sound very sure.

Turn the page! You never know about magic.

Jennie quickly turned the page. On the next page Sam saw a furry white dog sitting beside a pharaoh's throne. The dog sat stiff and straight, its hair drooping over its eyes.

Sam sat up straight, like the dog in the picture. *I would be a terrific royal dog.*

She caught sight of herself in the mirror and turned sideways to get a better look. She stuck her chin high in the air like Akasheput.

Jennie giggled. "Sam's pretending she's a royal dog."

Beth grinned as Sam posed for the mirror. "You'd be wonderful, Sam. Any king would want you."

Of course. Sam lifted her chin a little higher and looked straight into the mirror.

She froze. *Uh-oh. Maybe I'm too good looking.*

Jennie watched Sam's expression change. "What's wrong?"

Sam turned to Jennie. *I just had a terrible thought.*

"What is it?"

Promise me you won't panic.

"I promise."

Sam took a deep breath. *I think Menopharsib may have already spotted me.*

"You're just trying to scare us, Sam." Jennie picked up a red pencil and went back to her title page.

Beth looked up, curious. "If Sam's talking about the curse, she doesn't have to worry. We didn't rob his tomb."

Tell Beth he's after me. I saw him.

"Menopharsib is not after you." Jennie was firm.

You're wrong. Closing her eyes, Sam pictured

the snowy street and the lumpy gray figure coming through the snow. She stared hard at Jennie. *I know I'm right. I saw something.*

With a sinking feeling in the pit of her stomach, Jennie listened as Sam told her about the strange worm thing, and how it had looked at her.

Ask yourself, Jennie. Why would a big worm come toward me?

"What are you two talking about?" cried Beth. "You're having a conversation and I can't hear it!"

Taking a deep breath, Jennie told Beth what Sam had seen.

Beth thought for moment. "It makes sense," she said at last. "The mummy is out looking for his dog. And Sam looks like Akasheput." She started to chew a fingernail.

It was him. I know it.

Jennie twisted a long piece of her hair like she always did when she was worried. "I don't think it was him," she said hopefully. "Anyway, even if it was, he'll find another dog he likes better."

He won't like anybody better than me. Sam turned back to the mirror with a woeful face. *How could he? I'm beautiful ... and smart. Don't forget smart.*

"But there's lots of white furry dogs around," insisted Jennie.

Not like me. Sam's mind was racing. *I'm in big trouble here, Jennie.*

This dog-mummy thing is bad news.

8. Menopharsib Walks

That night Sam found another piece of beef jerky on the porch. *Love that mailman!*

While she watched the cars wind their way through the wintry streets, she sat down on the cold cement and chomped happily.

The night was icy dark, and the wind howled. The wind seemed to speak of the ancient priests and the magic of Menopharsib. Sam shuddered. *Jennie should listen to me. Everyone knows you can't escape a mummy.*

Just then Sam's ears pricked up. She heard a sound from the street.

Mmmmm ...

She listened.

Mmmmm … Mmmmm …

Sounds like some kind of chant.

Mmmmm … Mmmmm … Mmmmm …

Like those old priests chanting their evil spells.

Sam looked up and down the street but there was nothing. Only cold, snow and darkness.

Yikes! Maybe it's Menopharsib!

Sam shrank back behind the porch railing.

Mmmmm … Mmmmm … Mmmmm …

It's coming closer!

Mmmmm … Mmmmm … Mmmmm …

It is Menopharsib! If he sees me, he'll grab me!

Mmmmm … Mmmmm … Mmmmm …

I don't want to be locked up in his crummy tomb!

Sam scratched wildly on the door.

"Wait a minute, Sam," Joan called from inside.

Wait a minute! Sam scratched harder. *Are you kidding? Open up!*

Scratch. Scratch. *This is an emergency!*

Bob opened the door and scowled. "Don't wreck the door, Sam!" he snapped.

But Sam shoved past him and dashed up the

stairs. She leaped up on the spare bed and burrowed under the pillow.

Downstairs she could hear Bob's angry voice. "This is the last straw. Sam has to go to obedience school."

I used to think obedience school was the worst thing that could happen to me.

Now I know better.

Beth and Jennie were shocked when Sam told Jennie about the humming.

It was him, Jennie! You have to believe me!

"It couldn't be him," Jennie frowned and looked over at Beth. "C-could it?"

"It had to be him." Beth's freckles stood out on her nose.

Jennie turned pale. "I d-don't think he'd look for Akasheput in Woodford." Her voice was small.

"Of course he would, Jennie!" shouted Beth. "He followed us back from the museum trip!"

Beths's right. Think about it, Jennie.

Sam paced back and forth. *Just imagine you're on a nice journey to the afterlife and suddenly your dog's gone. Then you get moved to a museum across the ocean and you're not even in your own tomb anymore. Then a whole bunch of kids stare at you and make stupid jokes. And all you want is peace and quiet because you're dead ...*

Sam looked up at Jennie. *Any mummy would get mad.*

Jennie gulped. "Sam thinks M-Menopharsib has some stuff to be m-mad about."

Some stuff! Sam grunted. *He has loads of reasons!*

Jennie looked worried.

"Sam's right! I bet he's furious!" Beth bit her fingernails fiercely. "I wish we hadn't gone to see him. He knows where to find us!"

I wish you two would listen. He found us already! And he's chanting up a new spell.

Jennie blinked. "A n-new spell?"

Sure. That's what the humming was. It was one of those magic chants.

I'd know that sound anywhere.

9. Menopharsib in Woodford

The masked faces of the ancient priests hovered over Sam. "Mmmmmm," they chanted as the huge knife glinted in the flickering light.

Sam's skin crawled. She couldn't move. She was tied down on a stone altar! The knife was coming closer!

A bull mask leered at her. Only the eyes behind the mask were alive — black and beady and evil.

A bird mask crowded in behind it. Bright eyes peered through the holes in the mask.

"Mmmmmm," it chanted.

Help! Help! But no one could hear. Sam tried to growl, but no sound came out.

Closer and closer came the terrible knife. *He's going to make me into a dog mummy!* Sam scrunched her eyes shut. *And he's going to trap me in a deep, dark tomb under the pyramids — forever.*

"Mmmmm ..."

Sam struggled. Panting, she stared out into sudden blackness. She waited for the flash of the knife. But nothing came.

Then she sniffed. *What's this?* The smell was familiar. *I'm home! I'm on the spare bed where I belong!*

Sam flopped back on the pillows. The priests were gone. *Whew! I must have been dreaming.*

She lay in the darkness thinking about her dream. *No problem. I'm alone in here ...*

Suddenly an odd tingly feeling slithered up and down Sam's spine. *Wait a minute.* She held her breath. *I feel like there's somebody in here with me. Maybe that mummy got in ...*

Yow! She burrowed under the covers and wriggled down to the bottom of the bed. She felt as if the mummy's cold hand was reaching through the darkness to grab her. Her skin crawled. *One minute I'm in a dream. The next minute that mummy's in my house!*

Sam put her paws over her head and huddled under the covers, afraid to move.

It's the magic!

Nothing can stop magic.

The next day seemed to last forever. Sam was afraid to nap. *I don't want to dream about that knife again.*

Hour after hour dragged by. She paced — past the kitchen, through the living room, up the stairs, down the stairs, on the spare bed, off the spare bed.

The clock ticked loudly in the empty house. *Shut up, clock. I've got a mean mummy hunting me down. I don't want to listen to your dumb noise.*

Sam growled, but the clock ticked on.

She jumped up on the sofa and looked outside. *Phooey. No cars. No people. Just snow.*

Just then Sam saw a movement out of the corner of her eye. Around the corner came the strange, lumpy worm thing.

Uh-oh.

Sam watched it stride briskly down the other side of the street. She squinted to get a better look. *Hmm ... bumpy looking ... grayish ... no hair ... no face ... You can't see his eyes ...*

Sam's skin crawled. *I wish Jennie and Beth could see this. It's Menopharsib!*

He's wearing a ski suit so nobody will scream. That's why he looks so lumpy. It's the bandages underneath!

He's wearing a mask ... and something over his head so you can't see the bandages ... and goggles so you can't see his dead mummy eyes ... Even his hands are wrapped up.

Nice disguise, Menopharsib.

To Sam's horror, Menopharsib stopped across from her house. She gasped. He was turning! He aimed his round goggles right at Sam!

She ducked. *Go get another dog. Buzz off back to*

ancient Egypt.

She waited. Then very carefully, she peeked up over the back of the sofa. What she saw made her heart stop!

Menopharsib was crossing the street! He was coming straight toward Sam's house!

When he reached the sidewalk, he raised a lumpy hand. He was waving at Sam!

Oh, no! Sam rolled off the couch and crouched on the floor.

He's trying to tell me something!

After a minute she raised her head slowly. Menopharsib had walked even closer to her window. And he was still waving!

Yikes! Sam crouched down and squeezed under a lamp table. *He's waving as if he likes me.*

Uh, oh. He's decided I'm Akasheput.

She put her paws over her head. *I know what he's doing.*

He wants me to know he's coming to get me!

10. Sam Needs Help

HE SPOTTED ME!

When Sam heard Jennie's key in the lock, she bounded to the door. She told Jennie that Menopharsib was walking around in a gray ski suit so nobody would see his rotten bandages.

Jennie gasped. "Are you sure it was him?"

Sam nodded. *Yup.*

Sam fixed Jennie with a hard look. *It gets worse, Jennie.*

"It does?"

He stared at me. Then he waved.

Jennie could feel panic rising in her chest. "M-maybe it wasn't him. We have to k-keep calm, Sam."

Some dead mummy waves at me and you want me

to keep calm?

"Well … I'd rather t-talk about it when Beth gets here."

Sam gave Jennie a long look. Then she shrugged. *Okay. I'll look for one of the mailman's treats.*

They looked on the porch for the beef jerky, but they couldn't find any. Sam stared dolefully at the ice. *I haven't had beef jerky for two days.*

"That's weird." Jennie looked in all the corners. "The mailman comes every day."

Sam sniffed one last time. *I'll look again tonight.*

Jennie shuddered. "Maybe you shouldn't come outside alone."

But I love beef jerky.

"I think you should stay inside."

Phooey. I get one little treat in my boring life and you don't want me to have it.

Sam sat down with a thud. *I'm bored and I'm starving.* She looked up at Jennie sadly. *I've told you to call the Humane Society about my life, but you never do.*

Sorrow washed over Sam. *Now there's a mean mummy after me and you won't even talk about it.*

Jennie's brown eyes softened. "Let's go to my house."

Will you give me a good snack?

Jennie started to say that Sam should eat dog food but stopped herself. They could talk about dog food later. She smiled at Sam. "I promise."

Sam was still grumbling as she picked her way across the snow. She hated the way snow stuck between her toes. *Speaking of my terrible life ... Have you noticed that nobody's bothered to get me some boots?*

Jennie opened her front door and held it for Sam. "I've got nachos."

Phooey. You said a good snack.

"Nachos with cheese sauce?"

Double phooey.

Sam marched into the kitchen. *I want*

barbecue chips with lots of butterscotch sauce, chocolate cake with ketchup, and a nice jam and watermelon sandwich.

Jennie scurried around the kitchen looking for snacks. Upstairs in her bedroom she shut the door and spread nachos and bacon chips on the floor.

Sam sniffed. *This isn't what I asked for.*

"I'll get you something better tomorrow," Jennie promised.

Sam sighed as she lay down to nibble. *Well, at least it's food.*

When Beth arrived, Jennie told her that Menopharsib had waved at Sam again.

Sam shot Jennie a quick look. *Oho! So you do believe it's him!*

Jennie didn't answer. She looked pale and worried.

"That's terrible!" Beth gasped. "That means

he's after you! He thinks you're Akasheput!"

Sam gulped. *Tell me something I don't know.*

Biting her fingernails, Beth paced back and forth. "We have to think of something fast!"

Jennie sank into a chair. "Let's not talk about this. Maybe he'll go away."

Sam glared at her.

"I read something about an ancient potion that would make a mummy rest in peace." Beth paced faster. "But I don't remember where."

Hurry up and find it.

Suddenly Beth stopped. "Oh-no! We can't look for it now!" she moaned. "We have to finish our projects today!"

Sam groaned. *Tell me you're kidding.*

But Jennie breathed a sigh of relief and started digging in her schoolbag for paper.

You two are a big help. Sam climbed on the bed and threw herself down.

"Miss Chong says we have to hand in our projects tomorrow, Sam," explained Jennie.

I don't believe this. Sam glared as Jennie and Beth set out their pencils. *You're terrible friends.*

"I promise we'll look for the book when we're finished." Jennie cut a piece of paper carefully.

Sam's big head drooped. *I've got a rotten mummy after me and nobody cares.*

"Of course we care, Sam." Jennie started to trace a picture. "We'll stay inside where it's safe."

Sam rolled over and faced the wall. *You two should be looking for the book that tells about the potion.* She sighed. *This is the first time reading would be any use. And you can't be bothered!*

"We can too be bothered!" Jennie answered hotly as she underlined her title.

Beth was writing. "I wish I could remember what book I read that in."

Jennie started to cut out her picture.

Sam lifted her head. *Excuse me. I hope it's not too much trouble to save my life here.*

"Sam, I have to finish my project," explained Jennie.

I should bite.

Jennie put her scissors down. "I give up. We

have to look for the book now. Sam says she's going to bite."

Beth hooted.

Sam fixed her gaze on Beth. *Tell this kid to find the book. Menopharsib is hanging around my house, and I need to put him to sleep.*

"Okay. Okay." Jennie threw up her hands. "Sam wants to get the mummy back to sleep right now."

"Can't we finish our projects?"

Humans are so selfish. No wonder they make mummies out of each other. Sam growled at her friends.

Beth giggled and set down her pencil. "Okay, Sam. We're looking."

Beth started leafing through books. "It was a story about some kids who put a mummy back to sleep," she muttered as she turned page after page. "They found an ancient potion in an old book and it worked."

Jennie picked up another book and started flipping through it.

The hair over Sam's eyes moved up and down

as she watched. *Hurry up.*

I'm a very beautiful dog.

That guy won't stop until he gets me.

11. The Magic Potion

After supper that night, Sam whined until Joan opened the front door and let her out.

Sam looked up and down the snowy street. No one was around. She sniffed around the porch for the lovely smell of beef jerky.

Then she heard a sound.

Mmmm … Mmmm …

Not this again.

Mmmm … Mmmmm … Mmmmmm …

It's him!

Sam didn't wait. She dove at the door and scratched.

The door opened instantly. "Stop scratching!" snapped Joan. "You're ruining the door!"

From the street came the humming sound. Mmmmm …

Sam dashed upstairs and crawled under the spare bed, her heart pounding wildly.

Jennie's right. It's not safe out there.

Sam's night was filled with horrible dreams. Evil chanting, deep stone rooms and long knives flitted through her mind as she huddled under the spare bed.

At last the morning sun shone through the window.

Jennie and Beth better find that book today.

I'm running out of time.

The next day after school, Beth burst through the door with a book in her hand. Sam saw the picture of a mummy on the cover.

"I knew I read it somewhere!" Beth crowed, waving the book.

Sam's spirits soared. *Yes!*

"It's in here, Sam!" cried Jennie, her eyes shining.

Tell me. Tell me.

Beth ran her finger down a page. "In this story the kids mixed some stuff and boiled it on the stove."

Jennie peered over Beth's shoulder. "And then they put the mixture near the mummy case!"

The what?

"The mummy case. It's a coffin with the dead guy's picture painted on it."

Beth turned the page. "Look! This mummy never got up again."

That's what I want.

"Let's get started on the potion," Jennie said.

"Hey!" cried Beth. "We have to go back to the museum to put it near Menopharsib's mummy case!"

Jennie's face fell. "How can we do that?"

Beth set her jaw. "We'll find a way." She crossed her arms firmly. "First we'll make the stuff."

What's in it?

"What do we need, Beth?"

Beth read: "Pine gum, pomegranate seeds, crushed grape seeds, orange pieces and honey." She was silent for moment, then she read on: "Boil together on a moonless night. Pour into honeycomb, then place it near the mummy case so the mummy will rest."

Jennie twirled a strand of her brown hair thoughtfully. "What's honeycomb?"

Beth shrugged.

"And what are pomegranate seeds?"

Beth shrugged again. "No idea."

They fell silent for minute.

"The dictionary!" cried Jennie, grabbing a huge book off a shelf.

Jennie flipped page after page. "P," she muttered. "P-O ... Here it is." She jabbed the book with her finger. "Pomegranate — a large, reddish, tough-skinned fruit that grows on a tree."

"Where will we find those?" asked Beth.

A store, of course.

"The supermarket," said Jennie. "They have everything."

Jennie flipped the pages again. "Honeycomb ... H ... Here it is. Honeycomb — the wax cells built by bees to store their honey."

Beth snapped her fingers. "I've seen that! It's like little boxes stuck together and filled with honey. The store will have it."

You two get the stuff. I'll watch the moon.

Jennie looked at Beth. "But how will we get back to the museum?"

"Let's make the potion." Beth looked very determined. "Then we'll figure out how to put it near Menopharsib's case."

Things are looking up.

The next day Jennie and Beth rushed in after school carrying a bag from the supermarket.

"We got everything, Sam!" cried Jennie.

She pulled out a hard, reddish ball a with

little tuft on the bottom. "This thing is a pomegranate."

Sam eyed it curiously. *Looks like cardboard. How do you bite it?*

"The lady at the supermarket said you cut it open and eat the juicy parts inside."

Sounds gross.

Then Beth pulled out some waxy, gunky stuff in a plastic tray. "This is honeycomb."

Sam sniffed. *Yuck.*

"All we have to do is boil everything together and pour it into the honeycomb." Beth's green eyes shone happily. "Simple."

"Yeah. But I still don't know how we'll put it near his mummy case," objected Jennie.

Beth held up her hand. "I have the perfect plan. I'll ask to go to the museum for my birthday. My mother's been asking me what I want."

Beth is such a great kid. Sam gave Beth a huge slurp.

Beth patted Sam's big head. "Relax, Sam. We'll put that mummy back to sleep, and you won't have a thing to worry about."

Sam heaved a sigh of relief. *Make it fast. Worrying makes me crabby.*

12. The Mummy Knows

Every night Sam looked out the spare-room window, and every night the moon got thinner.

One night the moon was a sliver. The next night it was smaller still. On the third night there was no moon at all.

After supper Jennie came to get Sam. They stood in Jennie's backyard and looked up at the starry, black winter sky.

See? No moon.

"I'll call Beth. Come on, Sam." Jennie ran inside.

"No moon," Jennie breathed into the phone. "Ask your mother if you can come over tonight. My parents are going to a meeting."

"Wait a minute," came Beth's voice.

Jennie held her breath while Beth talked to her mother.

Beth came back. "No problem. My dad will drive me."

"Great. Noel's baby-sitting."

"How are we going to do anything with him around?"

"Don't worry. He'll ignore us," said Jennie.

Tell that big lummox not to get in the way.

Jennie grinned at Sam. "I'll tell him."

"See you soon." Beth hung up the phone.

Sam and Jennie went up to Jennie's bedroom.

A few minutes later, Jennie's mother poked her head in the door. "We're going now, Jennie. Noel will take Sam home before nine."

I don't want that big oaf taking me anywhere.

"Noel has a lot of homework," Jennie's mother continued. "So you and Beth and Sam will have to be quiet."

"We won't bother him," Jennie promised.

Just then the doorbell rang. "Good. That's

Beth," said Mrs. Levinsky. "Now, no noise. I want Noel to study."

Who cares about studying? We have more important stuff to do.

When her parents were gone, Jennie rummaged under her bed for the grocery bag. Then she peeked into Noel's room. In a flash she was back. "He's busy," she hissed. "Come on."

Very quietly the three friends tiptoed down to the kitchen.

Jennie got out the cutting board and cut the pomegranate into sections. Then she started picking out the bright red bits.

Beth poured the honey from the honeycomb into a bowl.

Hey, Jennie, maybe you should turn out the lights.

"Do you think we have to do this in the dark, Beth?" asked Jennie.

Beth thought for minute. "The story said no

moon. It didn't say anything about lights." She started chopping oranges.

Jennie popped clumps of pomegranate into the blender. "I wonder how much of this you need," she muttered.

Lots. I want that guy knocked out cold.

Suddenly Noel poked his head around the kitchen door. "Are you kids making a mess?"

Buzz off. We never make messes.

Jennie jumped. "Um … We're doing a project for school."

"Yeah." Beth looked up from the chopping board. "We have to make something."

Noel sidled over to the counter and picked up the grapes.

Don't touch, Lummox. You'll bring us bad luck.

"Don't eat this stuff, Noel," objected Jennie. "It's for school."

Noel narrowed his eyes as he popped a grape into his mouth. "I never had to do this when I was your age."

"Miss Chong told us to do it," Jennie insisted.

"What's it for?" Noel ate two more grapes

and spat out the seeds.

"We're studying ancient Egypt," offered Beth. "This is what they ate."

Noel picked up the pomegranate. "What's this stupid-looking thing?"

Jennie grabbed it. "It's a pomegranate. The ancient Egyptians ate them all the time."

Noel picked red bits out of the pomegranate and nibbled. "Weird."

You're the one who's weird. Sam glared at Noel. *Tell him to go away.*

"Go away, Noel," repeated Jennie firmly. "We have work to do."

"If you make a mess," Noel complained, "Mom will blame me."

Good. Let's make a huge mess.

Jennie giggled.

Noel looked at them suspiciously. "I have to call my girlfriend," he said. "No mess."

Lucky girl.

At last Noel was gone.

Bye, bye, Lummox.

"Whew!" said Jennie. "Did you ever see

anybody as nosy as him?"

"Never." Beth watched as the blender swirled pomegranate berries into a red mush.

Jennie picked seeds out of the grapes, while Beth poured the pomegranate mush into the honey. Then they blended the grape seeds and the orange pieces and mixed it all together in sticky lumps.

Beth pulled a plastic bag out of her jeans pocket. "Pine gum. I scraped it off our trees." She stared at the hard gray glop sitting at the bottom of the bag. "Maybe we should melt it in the microwave."

Jennie nodded.

Beth put the pine gum on a dish and popped it in the microwave.

After two minutes, Jennie scraped the goo into the mixture and stirred. Nothing mixed together.

"Put it all in the microwave," suggested Beth.

"This stuff is yucky," complained Jennie as she tried to scrape the bowl. She put it in the microwave and watched it bubble. "I'm afraid it'll catch on fire. Better pour it into the honeycomb now."

Beth poured. It plopped out of the bowl in a big blob.

"This is disgusting," muttered Beth as they scraped the stuff off the counter and mashed it into the honeycomb in sticky globs.

Jennie suddenly felt suspicious. "Why would this stuff put a mummy back to sleep? It doesn't make sense."

It's magic. Magic isn't supposed to make sense.

Beth looked at the gooey mess. "It's a spell," she said firmly. "That's why it works."

I love Beth.

Tossing and turning on the spare bed, Sam couldn't stop thinking about food.

At last she could stand it no longer. *I have to get some beef jerky. I don't care how dangerous it is outside.*

Padding down the stairs, she went straight to the front door and whined until Joan let her out.

Sniffing around the porch, she found another piece of beef jerky under the snow. Just as she started chewing, she pricked up her ears.

A long, low hum echoed down the street. Mmmm … Mmmmm …

In horror, Sam dropped the beef jerky on the icy porch. *It's him again! He's come to get me!*

Sam scratched wildly on the door.

Instantly it opened and Bob shouted, "Stop wrecking this door! You bad, bad dog!"

Sam shoved past him. *That mummy knows we've got the potion. I'm doomed.*

She shot up the stairs, leaving Bob shouting after her.

It's not the mailman who's leaving me the beef jerky!

She burrowed under the covers and crawled to the bottom of the spare bed.

Menopharsib's leaving it!

13. He's Coming to Woodford

"Sam thinks Menopharsib is leaving the beef jerky on her porch!" cried Jennie the next day.

Beth gasped. "That means he has a plan."

"A p-plan?"

"Nobody leaves beef jerky for a dog unless they have a reason." Beth was grim. "I bet he's trying to get Sam outside."

Beth folded her arms and looked at Sam. "Don't go out on the porch, Sam. No matter how hungry you get."

But I love that stuff.

"Forget the beef jerky, Sam," snapped Jennie.

"This is serious."

"Maybe it's got a magic spell on it," mused Beth. "Sam says every time she starts to chew she hears the mummy chanting. Right?"

Sam's head whipped up. *Yeah. That's right.*

Jennie bit her lip unhappily.

That's it, Jennie! It's one of those ancient spells. As soon as I touch the stuff, he appears!

"Maybe it is magic," agreed Jennie nervously.

"Stay inside, Sam," ordered Beth. "And don't touch that beef jerky no matter how good it smells."

So what am I supposed to do for food?

Jennie looked narrowly at Sam. "It could be poison. Remember he wants you for a dog mummy."

Poison!

Sam slumped down with a thud.

Why did he have to mess with my beef jerky?

He can do whatever he wants to the Liver Delight.

With a shout, Beth and Jennie burst through Sam's door after school the next day.

"You're not going to believe this!" shouted Jennie. Kicking off their snow boots, she and Beth did a little dance in the front hall.

Sam glared from the sofa. *The mummy waved at me again today, in case anybody cares.*

But Beth and Jennie twirled around the room gleefully.

"It's the best news!" sang Jennie happily.

Sam rolled her eyes.

Beth did a few turns around Jennie. "You'll love this, Sam."

Sam glared harder. *I'm turning into a dog mummy here, and all you two do is dance.*

"We can't get to the museum, Sam," sang Jennie happily.

Sam gasped. *If you're happy about that, I need*

new friends!

"But …" Jennie grinned at Sam.

Sam eyed Jennie suspiciously.

"… the museum is coming to us!" Jennie shrieked.

Yeah, right. Like I believe that.

"Tell her, Beth." Jenny twirled around in glee.

"The museum is bringing a traveling display, Sam," explained Beth. "And they're bringing Menopharsib's mummy!"

Sam gasped.

Jennie grinned. "Miss Chong told us the exhibition arrives on Saturday!"

I hate Miss Chong. She's the one who got me into this mess.

Jennie giggled. "On Saturday we can put the mixture beside Menopharsib's mummy case, and your troubles are over."

She snapped her fingers in Sam's face as she whirled past.

"Just like that!"

14. A Dangerous Plan

"It's the luckiest thing that could have happened!" Beth grinned. "Who would have thought Menopharsib would come to Woodford?"

Sam scowled. *Sounds too lucky, if you ask me.*

Jennie stopped twirling. "It does seem a bit weird, doesn't it?"

Definitely weird.

A cold feeling was growing in Jennie's chest.

Nobody gets that lucky, Jennie.

"They don't?"

It's not luck.

Beth was watching Sam and Jennie closely. "What's Sam talking about?"

"She doesn't think this is luck, Beth."

Beth was suddenly worried. "You mean … it's part of the plan?"

Exactly. Menopharsib arranged it all.

Jennie nodded.

He's coming to get me.

Sam's heart started to pound. *The mummy has magic, Jennie! That means he can do anything he wants …*

Sam paced up and down the couch. *We'll have to work fast.*

I want that mummy in a coma.

The week dragged on. Sam thought Saturday would never come.

Every day the mummy waved at her through the living-room window. Every day Sam dove under the lamp table to hide. And every day she waited nervously until Jennie came.

Beth always came, too, with the magic

potion in a plastic bag. "I can't leave it at home," she explained. "My Mom will think it's just old gunk and throw it out."

As the week went by, Jennie and Beth found three more pieces of beef jerky on the porch.

Without even letting Sam have a sniff, the girls threw them in the garbage.

"We're not taking any chances, Sam," Beth said darkly.

Sam glared. *Just my luck.*

The yummiest snack in the world has some crummy spell on it.

At night, Sam couldn't stop worrying. They would have to put the potion beside the mummy case when the mummy was sleeping. If he was wandering around the town, he'd see them.

Thoughts tumbled through her head as she lay on the spare bed. In her mind she saw the mummy lurching down Main Street with wrappings trailing behind his lumpy feet. He had the magic of the ancient priests. As old as evil itself.

Rotten eyes peered out of the bandages ... eyes that would never let go. *Nothing can stop him. Not tanks. Not bullets. Not bombs.*

No one can escape.

15. Menopharsib Comes

On Saturday morning Sam woke up early. At last it was exhibition day! She walked to the window and looked out over the peaceful snowy streets of Woodford.

The town looked like a winter scene on a Christmas card. It was hard to believe that a terrible mummy was out there — waiting to grab her.

Sam shuddered and went downstairs.

At breakfast, she lurked under the table and listened to Joan and Bob crunch cereal. *This is crazy. They can eat whatever they want. Why don't they have something good for breakfast? Like chocolate cake with sardines.*

She eyed the disgusting mound of Liver Delight in her bowl. *Better still ... why don't they feed me chocolate cake and sardines?*

Just then the doorbell rang. It was time to go to the museum exhibition.

Outside, the sidewalk was covered with powdery, fluffy snow. The street was still and silent. As Sam trotted along beside Jennie and Beth, she shivered every time cold snow squished up between her toes.

Sam kept looking up and down the street.

"If we see Menopharsib, we'll just hide," whispered Jennie.

"Yeah," added Beth. "We'll run into somebody's backyard or something. Don't worry, Sam."

Who's worried? Sam whipped around to see if Menopharsib was behind them.

Where are we going anyway?

"To the library, Sam," explained Jennie. "The traveling exhibition is in a big trailer in the parking lot."

Without another word, the three friends crossed Main Street. As they rounded the corner, Sam saw the long trailer.

Jennie clutched at Beth's mittened hand. "I'm s-scared. Are y-you?"

Beth shrugged. "Sure I am. But we're not letting that mummy grab Sam." She held up the plastic bag with the potion in it. "This stuff better work."

"W-what if it doesn't?"

"It'll work," said Beth grimly. "The book said so."

From outside, the traveling exhibition looked like an odinary trailer, long and low with wooden steps leading up to the door. A big sign with a pyramid on it said

EGYPTIAN EXHIBITION. The parking lot was empty.

So, where is everybody? Sam looked up and down the street. *Hmmm ... I hope this doesn't mean he got up early.*

Jennie put her foot on the first step. "I-I-I don't want to go in."

"I do." Beth marched up the stairs. "Follow me. We'll put this stuff beside his mummy case and we'll be out in five minutes."

Reluctantly, Jennie followed Beth up the stairs. Beth pushed the door and peeked in.

Inside, a tired-looking guard was doodling on a paper. He hardly looked up. "Come on in," he said. "We've just opened. You have the whole place to yourselves."

Beth and Jennie tiptoed in. Sam shoved past them. *Let me see.*

The guard glanced at Sam. "I don't know about the dog," he said, doubtfully.

"She'll be good. We promise," pleaded Jennie.

Come on, buddy. This is life and death here. Don't slow me down.

"Well ..." said the guard slowly. "Since there's nobody here yet, I guess it'll be all right." He looked straight at Jennie. "But you have to keep your dog under control. Any trouble and you're out."

Okay. Okay. We get the picture.

"She'll be perfect," promised Jennie.

"She's always perfect," added Beth.

"She better be." He pointed to an arrow on the wall. "Start over there. The signs will tell you everything you need to know about each exhibit." Then he went back to his doodling.

Their hearts in their throats, Jennie, Beth and Sam moved past displays of pottery, tools, clothing, a model of a pyramid and then ...

They stopped so suddenly they piled into each other. At the far end of the trailer, straight ahead, was a mummy case. It stood on stone legs, just like the pictures they'd seen. On the wall behind it was an eerie painting of priests and fires and mummies.

Sam could feel something coming at her from the mummy case. Waves of evil rolled toward her. She felt Menopharsib's breath on her face — hot and rotten — and she thought she heard a humming sound. He was chanting!

Sam could hardly breathe. *Quick! Put the stuff over there!*

Jennie and Beth held on to each other and started toward the mummy case.

Sam shoved into Jennie's legs. *Hurry up! I want this guy out cold!*

The three friends moved closer.

Sam felt dizzy.

Closer …

Closer …

When they got to the mummy case, Beth leaned forward to peer through the glass.

"W-w-what are you doing?" Jennie hissed, tugging at Beth's sleeve.

Beth shook her hand off. "I want to be sure he's in there!" She leaned over to look. "We're safe. We've got the potion."

Sam stopped for moment and then jostled in behind them. *I want to see, too.*

Standing on her hind legs, Sam stood up

behind Beth and peered through the glass. There, inside the case lay a small wrapped mummy. Menopharsib was not as big as an ordinary man.

Hey! This guy can shrink himself! There's no end to his magic!

"Put the potion d-down, Beth," Jennie whispered. "Let's go home!"

Beth carefully placed the plastic bag beside the glass case.

Sam chortled at the shrunken mummy. *There you go, bad guy. You're in a coma now! You didn't get me! Ha! Ha! Have fun in the afterlife with no dog! I bet —*

Sam reeled back. *Yikes! His eyes flew open!*

"No, they didn't," hissed Jennie.

Humans never see anything. I tell you, he's furious! Let's get out of here!

Sam ran for the exit door and crashed against it. *Come on! Let's go!*

"Hey!" shouted the guard from the front of the trailer. "I thought you said that dog was going to behave!"

I am behaving! The mummy's awake! I'm out of here!

Outside, Sam wheeled up a side street and dashed to the corner. Jennie and Beth thudded close behind.

"What's going on?" puffed Beth.

"Sam says Menopharsib's eyes flew open!" panted Jennie.

Beth looked around in horror.

The back of Sam's neck prickled. *Hurry!*

Without speaking, they scurried along the snowy sidewalk. The swoosh of every passing car made them jump. Menopharsib was watching them from somewhere with his magic!

"That is so weird," Beth muttered as they darted across Main Street and headed for Sam's house. "I didn't see his eyes open." But she kept looking back over her shoulder just in case.

Without slowing down, Jennie glanced back, too. "Neither did I."

I see things because I'm a great detective.

"Maybe it was Sam's imagination," wheezed Jennie, struggling through a snowdrift.

Sam gasped. *A good detective sees things other people are too dumb to notice.*

Sam growled under her breath. *Nobody appreciates me.*

Beth was thinking about what Jennie said. "Maybe his eyes did open."

You tell her, Beth.

Anything can happen with magic.

16. He Was Here!

Hearts pounding, Sam, Jennie and Beth raced up Sam's front steps. Joan and Bob's car was gone.

"Good," said Jennie. "Nobody's home."

On the porch, Sam skidded to a stop. *He's been here!*

"How do you know?" Jennie fumbled with the key.

Beef jerky! Smell it!

"I don't smell anything."

Human noses are useless.

Sam sniffed the corner of the porch and stared up at Jennie. *There! Under that pile of snow.*

"Sam says she can smell beef jerky, Beth."

Jennie turned the key and the door opened. She glanced at the street to see if Menopharsib was coming.

"Don't touch it, Sam!" yelled Beth. "There might be a spell on it — or poison!"

Phooey. Sam marched into the house leaving a trail of snow across the floor.

Outside, Beth scraped away the snow and found the beef jerky. "This goes straight into the garbage," she muttered, as she hurried through the door.

In the living room, Sam hopped up on the couch. Her paws hung over the edge, dripping on the carpet.

"Joan's going to be mad about all this snow in here," said Jennie. "We have to clean it up."

Ask me if I care. Sam stuck her nose in the air. *Maybe the snow on the rug is your imagination.*

Sam glared at her friend. *When I'm a poor wrapped-up dog mummy, you can say I imagined everything.* She put her wet paws over her nose and settled down to sulk.

Jennie stroked Sam's back softly.

"I didn't see his eyes open. That's all. I thought maybe you imagined it. I didn't mean to hurt your feelings."

Sam sniffed and turned her head away. *Hmph.*

"I'm sorry, Sam. Please don't be mad."

Maybe some food would cheer me up.

Beth was looking out the window. "There's nobody coming, Jennie."

"Whew! That must mean the potion worked. The mummy must be asleep."

Sam's head whipped up. *Wait a minute! If he's asleep, who left the beef jerky?*

"Menopharsib probably left it yesterday."

Oh, no he didn't! I sniffed around the porch this morning.

Jennie felt as if a cold hand was squeezing her heart. "If you sniffed out there before we went to the exhibition, Sam ..." Her voice trailed off.

Beth narrowed her eyes. "There was no beef jerky on the porch this morning?"

Jennie nodded.

"Then he put it there when we were in the

library?"

Jennie nodded again. "He must have."

"But he was in his mummy case! We put him to sleep." Beth glanced anxiously out the window.

"I know." Jennie swallowed hard.

"So ... he was walking around while we were looking at him? It doesn't make sense." Beth chewed on a fingernail.

"I know."

Sam sat up and looked hard at Jennie, the hair over her eyes moving up and down. *I know what it means.*

Jennie's voice quivered. "What's it mean, Sam?"

Simple. It's the magic.

"Wh-what?"

Menopharsib can be in two places at once. This proves it.

Jennie slumped down on the couch beside Sam. "You're right, Sam. It is proof."

"Proof of what?" Beth looked around from the window, worried.

"It proves Menopharsib can be in two places at once."

"I get it. He leaves his body in the mummy case … and goes outside at the same time?" Beth's green eyes were wide. "How can he do that?"

Jennie shrugged miserably.

I keep telling you — he can do anything he wants.

Both girls looked fearfully around the room and out at the street.

"But the potion is supposed to stop him." Jennie chewed her lip anxiously.

"Maybe it only works with ordinary mummies. Ones who don't have special powers." Beth's freckles stood out on her pale face.

Exactly.

I think I need a snack.

17. Meeting Menopharsib

Neither Jennie nor Beth had realized how powerful Menopharsib's magic was. What if the potion couldn't stop him?

Any minute now that creep will come by and start waving at me. Just watch.

"Let's go to my house," said Jennie. "Maybe he won't look for you there."

As they crossed the snowy lawn, they all felt Menopharsib's eyes watching them through the trees. "I feel like he's everywhere," shuddered Jennie.

"Me, too," said Beth. They rushed up to Jennie's room, shut the door and pulled the curtains.

The afternoon went by slowly. Sam ate cookies and pretzels and chips. The girls played CDs, and they all drank pop.

They tried to forget about Menopharsib. The idea that he could go anywhere he wanted while he was also in his mummy case was too scary to think about.

Around three o'clock, Mrs. Levinsky poked her head in the bedroom door. "Joan and Bob called. They want Sam to get some exercise today. You've been shut up in this room for hours."

Jennie looked up from the CD cover she was reading. "She had lots of exercise this morning, Mom."

But Jennie's mother insisted. "Sam should be outside getting some fresh air. And so should you."

Forget fresh air. Tell her to go away, Jennie.

Jennie rolled her eyes. "I can't say that to my mother, Sam," she whispered.

Hmph. Well, tell her I don't want to go out.

"Sam doesn't want to go out."

But Mrs. Levinsky was firm. "She has to go whether she likes it or not. Joan and Bob will be back at five o'clock. I want you to take Sam for a walk before they get home."

Great idea. Let's just stroll outside and let Menopharsib grab me.

Beth and Jennie started to protest, but Mrs. Levinsky was shutting the door. "I'm going back to the drugstore to close up. While I'm gone, I want that poor dog to have a nice walk."

Nice walk! Is she crazy?

Jennie and Beth stalled as long as they could.

At four-thirty Jennie looked at Beth. "We can't wait any longer."

Beth nodded. "Time to go out, Sam."

Sam glared.

But the girls pushed her off the bed. *This is a bad idea.* Sam dragged her feet as they pulled her out the bedroom door. *Those old priests knew what they were doing with those magic spells.*

I'm telling you ... I'm toast. Dog mummy here I come ...

But Jennie kept pushing. "We have to take

you for a walk, Sam. You heard my mother."

This is a bad idea, if anybody cares.

"Let's take Sam to my house," suggested Beth. "We'll go fast."

One of these days I'm going to bite you two. Sam tried to dig her toenails into the carpet at the front door.

But Jennie and Beth pushed her through the door and shut it firmly. Sam sat down on the porch with a thud.

"We have no choice, Sam," pleaded Jennie.

"We'll go straight to my house," added Beth.

Jennie and Beth took a deep breath and dragged Sam to the street. Their hearts were thudding in their throats.

Phooey.

This is a bad, bad idea.

Jennie, Beth and Sam looked around fearfully. Thick snow was falling, and early twilight was creeping over the silent winter streets.

Their footsteps fell noiselessly on the snow-covered sidewalks. Every once in a while, a car crept past with its lights on. No one was out walking.

As they turned a corner, Sam tried one last time. *Okay. That's it. We've walked long enough. Time to go back.*

But Jennie and Beth kept going.

I can't believe my friends would do this to me.

"Let's hurry," said Jennie nervously.

"Yeah," added Beth. "Straight to my house. You'll be safe, Sam."

I'd better be. I want a big pizza when I get there. And cheese puffs and peanuts. It's major stress walking around when a mummy is looking for you.

"We'll be okay at Beth's house." Jennie tried to sound sure of herself.

"It'll take us ten minutes to get there," chimed in Beth. "No longer."

I wish grown-ups would mind their own business. Here I am outside, with a terrible mummy after me . . . all because some crummy adult thinks I need fresh air.

A car swooshed silently around the corner, its headlights sweeping the snow.

Porch lights flicked on.

In the distance a dog barked.

Snow settled on Sam's back and on the girls' woolen hats. The sky was gray and thick with falling snow.

Okay. It's been ten minutes. Beth's house is too far. Let's go back.

"I think we've walked long enough," agreed Jennie.

Beth shivered. "But we're almost there."

Sam shook the snow out of her eyes.

Uh-oh.

Sam squinted. A big shadow was moving toward them!

"It's okay, Sam," said Jennie, feeling Sam stiffen beside her. "It's just somebody on their way home."

It's him! Sam's heart started to thud. *Look how lumpy that shadow is! It's him!*

Jennie peered into the snow. "I-I d-don't think that's him."

The shadow came closer.

"That's not him," said Beth confidently. "Don't worry, Sam."

Don't worry! Is she crazy?

The shadow kept coming. Beth narrowed her eyes to see through the snow.

Closer ...

Jennie squinted. Snowflakes stuck to her lashes.

With a pounding heart, Sam peered into the twilight and falling snow.

Then they heard it!

Mmmmmmmm ...

Uh-oh!

A lumpy gray figure was walking toward them.

Frozen with fear, the three friends stared into the blizzard.

They could see a smooth white head and

round goggles where its eyes should be.

Mmmmmmmmmm ...

Menopharsib!

Jennie gasped and grabbed Sam.

Beth screamed. "It's him!"

Hide me! Hide me! Sam tried to squeeze behind the two girls.

The thing kept coming.

Closer ...

Closer ...

Then its arms reached out of the snow and grabbed at Sam.

Jennie and Beth screamed.

"Hello there," squeaked a high voice.

He disguises his voice!

Back off! Sam bared her fangs and snarled. "Woof! Woof! Woof!"

"Grr-r-r. Grr-r-r-r-r. Grr-r-r." Sam snapped her jaws wildly.

"Don't be scared," the creature crooned. "I love sheepdogs."

I bet you do! Snap! "Grr-r-r. Grrr-r-r-r. Woof!"

Jennie and Beth clutched each other in horror.

Sam lunged and danced and bucked around the sidewalk. *Don't touch! Hands off!* "Grrr-r-r-r."

She bit at the air and barked ferociously. "Woof! Woof! Woof!"

"Now, now." The figure pulled something out of its lumpy pocket. "Here's a nice treat."

"Don't eat it, Sam!" screamed Beth.

Beef jerky! It's got a spell on it! Get it away from me! "Grrr-r. Grrr-r. Woof!"

"Leave our dog alone!" screamed Jennie, trying to hang on to Sam.

"Go away!" yelled Beth, picking up a lump of snow and throwing it.

"Wait a minute!" said the thing. "I just told you — I love sheepdogs."

Well, go love another one!

Sam leaped in the air and twirled around. "Woof! Woof! Grrr-r-r!"

She lunged at the creature's toes. *Yuck! I can't bite this guy ... I'd get a mouthful of rotten bones.*

"Get away!" hollered Jennie.

"Leave us alone!" screamed Beth.

"Woof! Woof! Grr-r-r! Woof! Woof!"

Sam snapped crazily at the air. But she was careful not to let her teeth touch the mummy.

Just then a light fell over them.

A car stopped, and two people jumped out.

Uh-oh.

More mummies!

18. Sam Goes Crazy

BACK OFF, YOU MUMMIES!

"Grrr-r-r-r. Grrr-r-r-r. Woof! Woof!" *You can't get me, you rotten mummies!*

Jennie and Beth screamed and threw snow at all the mummies.

One of the mummies grabbed Sam by the collar. *Uh-oh!* Sam yanked and growled and snapped.

From far away, she heard Bob's voice. *Bob's here! Good! Get this big guy, Bob! He wants to make a dog mummy out of me!*

"Grr-r-r-r. Woof!"

Bob's voice grew louder in Sam's ears.

Sam stopped barking. She looked up. Bob was holding her collar. Joan was beside him.

Whew! I'm glad you came.

But Joan and Bob looked furious.

That's right. Be mad at this guy. He's a mean pharaoh from three thousand years ago.

"What's going on?" yelled Bob, hanging on tightly to Sam's collar.

Tell him, Jennie. And while you're at it, tell him to stop choking me.

"Just what do you think you're doing, Sam?" screeched Joan.

Speak up, Jennie.

"Is this your dog?" asked the high, squeaky voice.

Don't tell that guy anything.

"I'm ashamed to say she is," answered Joan.

"She certainly is badly behaved," said the mummy primly.

Joan put her hands on her hips and stared at the girls. "Jennie, Beth. What's gotten into this bad dog?"

Jennie and Beth stuttered and stammered about the curse of Menopharsib ... and his dog Akasheput ... and their school projects ... and the mummy …

The mummy pulled off its goggles and white ski mask.

"I'm not a mummy!" the creature cried. Its long hair fell around its shoulders. "My name is Marion Wutherspoon."

Jennie and Beth stared open-mouthed.

Sam peered through the snow. *Probably a lie … hard to tell.*

"I live three blocks from here," Mrs. Wutherspoon said. "I power walk to keep fit." She looked at Joan and Bob. "All I was trying to do was make friends with your dog!"

"K-keep fit?" stammered Jennie.

"We thought you were a mummy!" blurted Beth.

Mrs. Wutherspoon held up her ski mask and goggles. "I guess I do look a bit strange." She looked down at her lumpy gray ski suit. "This ski suit keeps me warm."

Sam squinted. *How do we know this isn't another disguise?*

"She looks real," whispered Jennie.

"Why do you wear the face mask?" asked Beth.

"Sunlight, my dear," answered Mrs. Wutherspoon easily. "Too much sun on the skin causes wrinkles."

"Why the goggles?" Beth asked curiously.

"To protect my eyes," said Mrs. Wutherspoon. "Goggles keep out snow and glare, so I don't squint so much. Squinting causes wrinkles, too."

She laughed and shook her fluffy hair. "I'm just an ordinary fitness fanatic, my dears," she said happily. "Not a mummy at all."

"Excuse me," Beth said politely. "But, what's the humming sound?"

Mrs. Wutherspoon chuckled. "That's just a little chant I use. Keeps up my concentration."

She fished in her ski-suit pocket and held out a piece of beef jerky.

But Jennie held on to Sam. "Don't touch it. It might not be safe," she hissed in Sam's ear.

Phooey. Sam looked around at Jennie. *Would someone please tell me why all the good stuff is poison?*

Mrs. Wutherspoon raised her eyebrows in surprise. "I've been leaving one of these on her porch every time I walk past."

Still Jennie held Sam.

"I love sheepdogs," Mrs. Wutherspoon crooned. "I used to have one. He was the nicest dog I ever had."

Well, I believe that.

But Mrs. Wutherspoon turned to Joan and Bob. "I must say, this one is very bad-tempered."

Joan and Bob glared at Sam. "Yes, she is," said Joan through clenched teeth.

Bad tempered? I'm not bad tempered! I've been under a lot of stress. I've had a mean mummy after me. I've had worries. How would you like to be a dog mummy? Let me tell you something, lady ...

Sam gave one last growl. *I'm not even slightly bad tempered.*

I'm a wonderful dog.

Everybody loves me.

19. Sam's Punishment

WE'LL JUST SEE ABOUT THAT!

Sam watched suspiciously as the lady fluffed her hair again and shook hands with Joan and Bob.

This weirdo's getting too friendly if you ask me.

Mrs. Wutherspoon seemed interested in the girls' projects. She asked a lot of questions about Menopharsib and Akasheput.

Watch what you tell her, Jennie. Don't forget the magic.

After she heard the story, Mrs. Wutherspoon smiled. "Aren't children's imaginations a wonderful thing."

Hmph. I bet mummies make themselves look like people so they can get away.

Sam narrowed her eyes and stared.

Something's funny here, Jennie.
Mark my words.

At last Mrs. Wutherspoon said good-bye and power walked off into the snow. She turned and waved happily at them.

Hmph. As soon as she's out of sight, she's going to turn right back into a mummy.

Joan and Bob got back in the car, and asked Jennie and Beth to walk Sam home. They both scowled at Sam.

Sam stared after the car. *They shouldn't be mad at me. They don't know how tricky mummies are!*

Jennie was stern. "Forget the mummy, Sam. Mrs. Wutherspoon looked like an ordinary person."

Don't take chances with magic.

"I'm not taking chances, Sam!" yelled Jennie. "That lady is not a mummy!"

Sam was calm. *It's a new disguise.*

"It's not a new disguise!"

Is too.

"Is not!"

"I don't think it's a disguise," said Beth thoughtfully. "She's a real person, Sam."

So where's the mummy then?

Jennie shrugged. "I don't know where Menopharsib is. Maybe he's gone to another town to look for a dog."

He would never want another dog after he saw me.

"I don't think Menopharsib is anywhere around here," said Beth. "We would have seen him."

Hmph.

In silence the three friends walked through the thick snow to Sam's house. Sam's mind whirled with pictures of rotten mummies and evil priests. *Phooey. Just when I thought I had him.*

At last Sam stopped and looked up at Jennie. *So, she's not Menopharsib after all, huh?*

Jennie shook her head. "Nope. Mrs. Wutherspoon's definitely not a mummy."

"Definitely not," chimed in Beth.

She sure looked like a mummy.

Sam thought for a moment. *So, hand over the beef jerky, then.*

Jennie pulled it out of her pocket and gave it to Sam. While her friends waited, Sam chomped and chewed and swallowed noisily.

Suddenly Sam scowled up at Jennie. *Tell me something.*

Whose bright idea was it to put all those lovely pieces of beef jerky in the garbage?

Joan and Bob were waiting at the end of Sam's driveway.

"Thank you for looking after Sam, girls," Joan said in a cross voice. "She is in huge trouble."

No lectures. I refuse to listen to lectures.

Joan and Bob frowned at Sam. "Bob and I have made a decision, Jennie." Joan folded her arms firmly.

Jennie squirmed.

"She is a very bad dog, barking and growling like that."

Time to move to another topic. This one is getting old.

"We are ashamed of her," added Bob.

Blah. Blah. Blah.

"She snarled like a wolf!" exclaimed Joan.

Wolf, huh? Sam lifted her head proudly. *I told you I was a very tough dog. That lady will think twice before she goes around scaring people again.*

"We've decided," Bob was saying.

Blah. Blah …

"We've decided, Jennie —" Bob paused to scowl at Sam.

What have you boring adults decided now?

Sam yawned. But Bob's next words hit her like a thunderbolt.

"Sam is going to obedience school."

She snapped her mouth shut. *Obedience school!* Sam sat down in the snow with a thud.

That's what you think!

Obedience school is for stupid dogs, not for a famous detective like me.

Other books available in the
Sam, Dog Detective series

Spying on Dracula
The Ghost of Captain Briggs
Strange Neighbors
Aliens in Woodford
A Weekend at the Grand Hotel
The Secret of Sagawa Lake